BUSH BABY, BUSH BABY, GO TO SLEEP!

Written by

S.F. Hardy

Illustrated by

FX and Color Studio

Copyright

Summary: After a long day on a Kenyan safari, Jabbar is supposed to be asleep, but his room is taken over by bush babies that want to play and party.

Library of Congress Control Number: 2020924841
ISBN 978-1-7321861-8-7 (hardcover)

Dedicated to, Tory, our busybody entrepreneur
who never seems to sleep.
Keep reaching beyond the stars, Sun;
I love you!
-Mom

After a long day on safari in Kenya, Jabbar's mom told him to go to bed, but he wasn't sleepy. So, he made a tent with his blanket, grabbed his favorite book and big flashlight, and read.

All of a sudden,
Jabbar heard something.
Tap. Tap. Tap.
He looked at the window.

"What kind of animal are you? Enormous eyes, staring at me!"

Then, Jabbar remembered, "You're Africa's smallest primate. I saw you sleeping in the tree nest today.

A BUSH BABY!"

"You can stay, but you have to read and then go to sleep."

The bush baby leaped onto the bed and happily agreed.

All of a sudden, Jabbar heard something. Stomp! Stomp! Stomp! The sound came from inside the house.

Stomp.

Jabbar whispered, "Bush baby, bush baby, go to sleep. Mama doesn't want to hear a peep."

The bush baby scattered under the bed and pretended to snore.
Zzzz. Zzzz. Zzzz.

Just as Mom turned off the lights and closed the door, down from the window tumbled more.

Two, three, four!
Three more bush babies making
clicking noises on the floor!

"You all can stay.
I'll read you to sleep.
But if Mom comes back
and sees you here,
you're going to
be in big trouble,
right along with me."

The bush babies folded
their ears, and all agreed,
jumping under the tent
to listen to Jabbar read.

All of a sudden, Jabbar heard something.

Bang! Bang! Bang!
Mom was knocking at the door.

Jabbar whispered, "Bush baby, bush baby, go to sleep. Mama doesn't want to hear a peep."

Mom asked, "Jabbar! Why aren't you asleep?"

"I'm reading myself to sleep, Mom." He hoped she didn't see the bush babies.

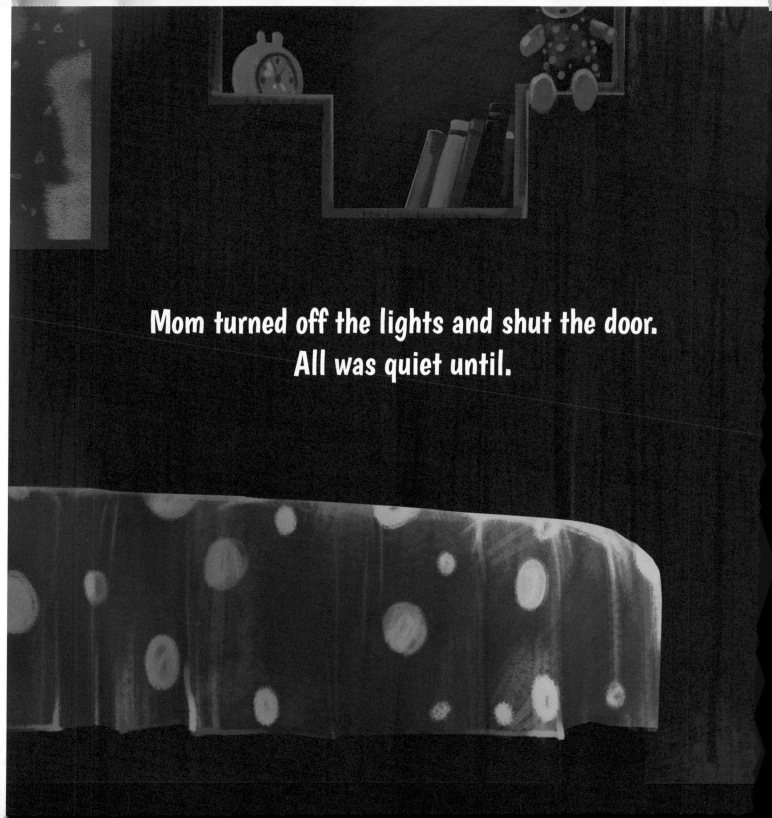

Mom turned off the lights and shut the door.
All was quiet until.

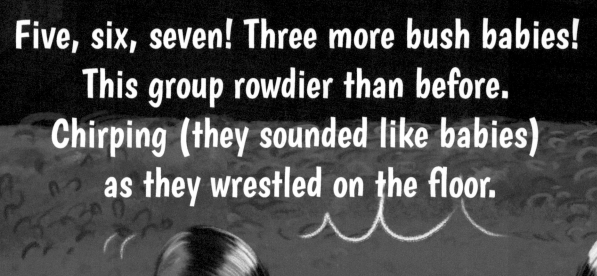

Five, six, seven! Three more bush babies!
This group rowdier than before.
Chirping (they sounded like babies)
as they wrestled on the floor.

All of a sudden, Jabbar heard something.
Shout! Shout! Shout!
Mom was coming back.
Jabbar whispered,

"Bush baby, bush baby,
go to sleep. Mama doesn't
want to hear a peep."

Mom yelled, "JABBAR! GO TO SLEEP!"
The bush babies ignored Jabbar's pleas and continued to play.
He opened the window to shoo them out, but there were more bush babies headed his way!

Eight, nine, ten!
That's enough! No more bush babies can come in.
"Put your glow sticks up and your radio too, so I can finish reading to you."

Jabbar whispered, "Bush baby, bush baby, go to sleep."

With a book in hand, Jabbar fell asleep, and the bush babies snuck out the window without making a peep.

Dear Family and Educators,

Thank you for choosing Bush Baby, Bush Baby, Go to Sleep!
We are excited for our reader's experiences as our mission is
to play a vital role in empowering children to be extraordinary
through literacy and active exploration. As such, we invite you to
go beyond your reading experience by engaging your youth
with the enclosed family/educator guide. This supplemental
resource will serve to enrich children's reading experiences,
while cultivating a joy for reading.

Enjoy!

S.F. Hardy and Shenomenal Ink

Discussion Questions:

1. What is another name for a bush baby?

2. Why do you think bush babies got the name, bush baby?

3. What countries, besides Kenya, can bush babies be found in?

4. What is the term used to describe animals
that are active at night?

5. What is the bush baby's habitat?

6. How do bush babies communicate with each other?

7. Approximately, how many bush baby species exist?

8. What is used to differentiate the various species of bush babies?

9. Do bush babies have predators? If so, what are they?

10. What continent does Kenya exist in?

11. What colors are in the Kenyan Flag?

12. There are 24 national parks in Kenya. Can you name two?

13. What countries surround Kenya?

14. What is a safari? Have you been on a safari? Would you like to?

15. Name one language spoken in Kenya?
Try Saying hello in the language you select.

16. Mwomboko is a popular dance in Kenya.
What does Mwomboko celebrate? Can you dance the Mwomboko?

17. Kenya is home to the world's fastest land animal.
What is the name of the animal?

Activities:

Word Challenge

Let's play a game! How many words can
you make out of the word Kenya?

Customize a Bush Baby Habitat

Help the bush babies get to sleep!

Here's what you need:
- ☐ 1 poster board (thin)   ☐ Glue
- ☐ Pencils   ☐ Crayons or markers
- ☐ Scissors   ☐ 1 piece of paper

Instructions:

1. Create a tree on the poster board by tracing
your hand for the branches.
2. Trace your arm for the tree trunk.
3. Cut your tree from the poster board.
4. Color the paper and cut it into thin strips of paper.
Glue strips together on the tree to make a nest.
5. Cut out bush babies from the back of your book and
place them in the tree. Read them to sleep.

Paper Puppet Play

1. Color and cut out bush babies provided.
2. Glue to a small piece of poster board.
3. Cut the poster board to the same shape as the bush baby.
4. Glue cutouts to popsicle sticks or clothespins (allow a few hours to dry completely).
5. While the glue is drying, create a fun play using facts from discussion questions.
6. Act play out once dry.
*You can use your puppets as bookmarks, too!

About the Author

S.F. Hardy reads until she falls asleep every night, a tradition her parents started when she was a little girl. Her mission as a children's librarian and literacy advocate is twofold—cultivate a joy for reading through early literacy initiatives and saturate the children's publishing market with books inclusive of marginalized people for everyone to enjoy!

Hardy, lives and creates in Detroit with her husband, son and cats, Violet and Milo.

More Books By S.F. Hardy
Dancing Monkeys In My Soup
Like A Salad
The Empress' New Hair

CPSIA information can be obtained
at www.ICGtesting.com
Printed in the USA
BVHW022200260221
601290BV00005B/7